Weasels with measles

Lesley Sims

Illustrated by David Semple

Wes and Lee, the twin weasels,
are painting their town

with dots, spots and splashes,
high up...

...and low down.

"It's so bright!" They grin with delight.
"Looks a treat!"

BEST
WOODLAND
STREET
CONTEST

JUDGING TODAY!

Brown Owl starts to scowl.
The twins look at their feet.

They quickly skip home,
two small spotty weasels.

"Oh no!" screams their mother,
"I think you have measles!"

"But Ma,
we are fine,"
Wes and Lee
try to say.

"Not one word.
Not a whine.
Head to bed.
Don't delay!"

She sends for
the doctor.

Hmm, spot
upon spot...

"Tongues out please. Say 'ahh'.
Now, do you feel hot?

There's no doubt about it.
These weasels have measles.

They may get quite snuffly
with sniffles and sneezles."

"If they wheeze or they sneeze,
let them eat some green cheese.

Please don't fret. It's the least
harmful weasel disease."

Ma lays a damp hanky on each little head.

But what's this? Both hankies have come away red.

"Thank goodness," says Ma,
in a whisper that's faint.

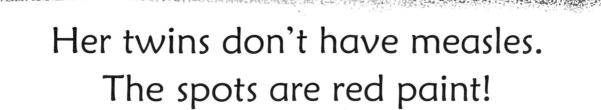

Her twins don't have measles.
The spots are red paint!

Just then, there's a 'Rat-a-tat-tat!'
and a shout.

"We want Wes and Lee.
Are they there? Send them out!"

"We've come first in the contest
for Best Woodland Street!"

"The judges said your spots
and splashes were sweet."

BEST WOOD

Everyone's dotty for the twins'
spots and dots.

LAND STREET

They throw them a party
with spots – lots and lots!

There's juggling and jam,
and those two jolly weasels...

...give everyone spots.
Now they've ALL got the 'measles'!

About phonics

Phonics is a method of teaching reading which is used extensively in today's schools. At its heart is an emphasis on identifying the *sounds* of letters, or combinations of letters, that are then put together to make words. These sounds are known as phonemes.

Starting to read

Learning to read is an important milestone for any child. The process can begin well before children start to learn letters and put them together to read words. The sooner children can discover books and enjoy stories and language, the better they will be prepared for reading themselves, first with the help of an adult and then independently.

You can find out more about phonics on the Usborne Very First Reading website, **www.usborne.com/veryfirstreading** (US readers go to **www.veryfirstreading.com**). Click on the **Parents** tab at the top of the page, then scroll down and click on **About synthetic phonics**.

Phonemic awareness

An important early stage in pre-reading and early reading is developing phonemic awareness: that is, listening out for the sounds within words. Rhymes, rhyming stories and alliteration are excellent ways of encouraging phonemic awareness.

In this story, your child will soon identify the long *e* sound, as in **neat** and **disease**. Look out, too, for rhymes such as **fine** – **whine** and **sneeze** – **cheese**.

Hearing your child read

If your child is reading a story to you, don't rush to correct mistakes, but be ready to prompt or guide if he or she is struggling. Above all, do give plenty of praise and encouragement.

Edited by Jenny Tyler
Designed by Sam Whibley

Reading consultants: Alison Kelly and Anne Washtell

First published in 2019 by Usborne Publishing Ltd., Usborne House, 83-85 Saffron Hill, London EC1N 8RT, England.
www.usborne.com Copyright © 2019 Usborne Publishing Ltd.